BENNO
and the NIGHt of
BROKeN
GLASS

In loving memory of Julia Thomas Ward. There is no friend
like a sister. — M.W.

The images in the afterword of this book are used with
the permission of: Yad Vashem, (Oranienburg Synagogue
in flames); © Hulton Archive/Getty Images, (a worker
clearing broken glass).

KAR-BEN PUBLISHING
A division of Lerner Publishing Group, Inc.
241 First Avenue North
Minneapolis, MN 55401 U.S.A.
1-800-4-Karben

Website address: www.karben.com

Library of Congress Cataloging-in-Publication Data

Wiviott, Meg.
    Benno and the Night of Broken Glass / by Meg Wiviott ; illustrated by
Josée Bisaillon.
        p.   cm.
    Summary: In 1938 Berlin, Germany, a cat sees Rosenstrasse
change from a peaceful neighborhood of Jews and Gentiles to an
unfriendly place where, one November night, men in brown shirts
destroy Jewish-owned businesses and arrest or kill Jewish people.
Includes facts about Kristallnacht and a list of related books and web
resources.
    ISBN 978-0-8225-9929-6 (lib. bdg. : alk. paper)
    1. Germany—History—1933-1945—Juvenile fiction.
2. Kristallnacht, 1938—Juvenile fiction. [1. Germany—
History—1933-1945—Fiction. 2. Jews—Germany—Fiction.
3. Holocaust, Jewish (1939-1945)—Germany—Fiction. 4. Cats—
Fiction.] I. Bisaillon, Josée, ill. II. Title.
PZ7.W7903Ben 2010
[E]—dc22   2008033482

Manufactured in the United States of America
4 – DP – 1/15/11

BENNO and the NIGHt of the BROKeN GLASS

Warsaw/Vickery Library

Meg Wiviott

illustrated by
Josée Bisaillon

KAR-BEN
PUBLISHING

Benno the cat lived at Number 5 Rosenstrasse in Berlin, just a few blocks from the Neue Synagogue. He had a nice warm bed near the furnace where Hans, the Hausmeister, left him fresh milk every night.

On Friday nights, Benno visited the Adler family in Apartment 3B. He watched Mrs. Adler light Sabbath candles, Mr. Adler slice a braided loaf of bread, and Sophie sing from a book she held close. After dinner, Sophie fed him scraps of chicken.

On Sundays after church, Benno visited the Schmidts, across the hall in Apartment 3A, for their family lunch. Before Mrs. Schmidt cleared the dishes for dessert, Inge sneaked bits of schnitzel to him under the table.

On weekday mornings, Benno watched Herr Adler and Herr Schmidt leave for work. He waited as Inge came out of her apartment and knocked on Sophie's door. Benno purred when the girls knelt to wish him *Guten Morgen*. Then he followed them to school.

During the day, Benno strolled around the neighborhood.

Sometimes Moshe the butcher fed him scraps and Frau Gerber, the grocer's wife, scratched his ears.

Often, he took naps nestled among the bolts of fabric in the sunny window of Mitzi Stein's dress shop.

In the late afternoons, Benno followed Inge and Sophie to the playground. He sat high in a tree as they played on the swings or dashed about in a game of tag with their friends.

Benno was welcomed by all, even into Apartment 2G, where Professor Goldfarb was too busy with his studies to pay attention when the cat curled up on his desk.

At night, Benno returned to his bed beside the furnace in the basement of Number 5 Rosenstrasse. He drank his milk and fell asleep listening to the comforting sounds of the **people above**.

Then things began to change.

Moshe the butcher had no scraps for Benno. Frau Gerber, the grocer's wife, had no time to scratch his ears. And Mitzi yelled, "Scat!" when Benno tried to nap in the window.

One night, men in brown shirts lit a bonfire on Rosenstrasse. As they threw books and papers onto the fire, the crowds cheered. Benno fled and tried to hide inside Apartment 2G, but Professor Goldfarb shooed him away. "I must save the books," the Professor muttered.

And a few days later, Benno watched Inge leave for school without knocking on Sophie's door. He waited a long time before Sophie came out and walked to school alone. Neither girl wished him *Guten Morgen*.

After school, Benno watched Inge with her friends at the **playground**. Sophie hurried **past** the **park**, her head low. Later, when Benno went home, he found the door to Apartment 3B locked.

Rosentrasse was still a busy street, but the people were no longer friendly. The men in brown shirts strutted about with their heads held high. Benno walked carefully, dodging their heavy black boots. The neighbors and shopkeepers went quietly about their business, their eyes lowered.

Then came a night like no other.
The air filled with screams and shouts,
sounds of shattering and splintering
glass, and the bitter smell of smoke.
Benno cowered in a doorway.

He watched the brown-shirted men
swarm over the neighborhood,
smashing windows and looting
shops. At Moshe's butcher shop, they
overturned the refrigerators, leaving
meat to spoil on the ground. At Mitzi
Stein's shop, they ripped the bolts of
fabric and threw the sewing machines
into the street.

Benno saw the beautiful Neue
Synagogue set ablaze. The Torah
scrolls were dragged into the street
and trampled.

Herr Gerber's grocery remained
untouched.

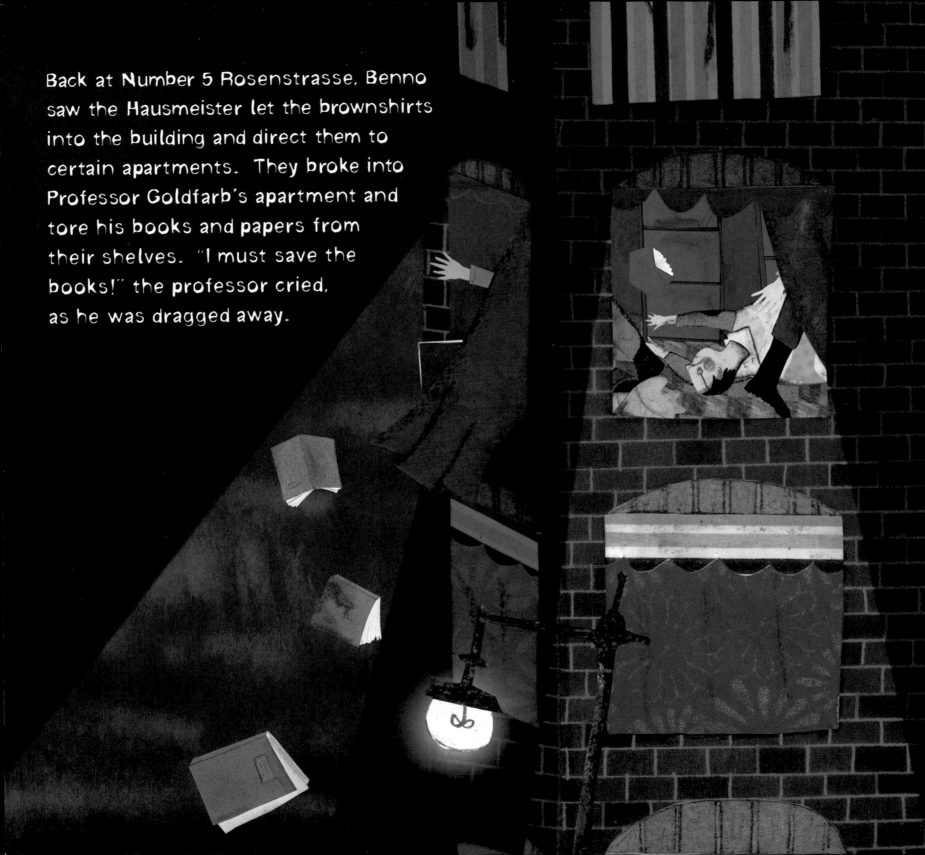

Back at Number 5 Rosenstrasse, Benno
saw the Hausmeister let the brownshirts
into the building and direct them to
certain apartments. They broke into
Professor Goldfarb's apartment and
tore his books and papers from
their shelves. "I must save the
books!" the professor cried,
as he was dragged away.

Benno ran upstairs. In Apartment 3B, the mob was breaking the Adlers' furniture and throwing books out the window, even the one Sophie sang from every Friday night.

The Schmidts' apartment was untouched.

The next morning, Benno saw Herr Schmidt leave for work.
Then Inge left for school.

He waited for Sophie, but the Adlers' door remained closed.

Outside, smoldering fires stung Benno's eyes. His paws were
cut and sore from the broken glass that littered the streets.

Smoke from the gilded dome of the Neue Synagogue rose into
the morning sky. Mitzi Stein was sweeping up the glass in
front of her store.

Herr Gerber's grocery was open for business as usual.

Benno could not find Moshe the butcher. He never saw
Professor Goldfarb or Sophie and her family again.

Benno continued to sleep
in his bed by the furnace.
Hans continued to give him
fresh milk, and Frau Gerber
scratched his ears. Benno
still watched Herr Schmidt
leave for work. He still
followed Inge to school.

But life on Rosenstrasse
would never be the same.

Afterword

For many, Kristallnacht (the Night of Broken Glass) marks the beginning of the Holocaust. Although the characters in this story are fictional, the setting and the events portrayed are real.

This pogrom, on November 9, 1938, was triggered by an assassination of a German official two days earlier. Joseph Goebbels, the Nazi Minister of Propaganda, used it as an excuse to unleash gangs of Nazi youth and Stormtroopers (brownshirts) to destroy Jewish shops, homes, and synagogues. The violence continued into the morning of November 10th.

Approximately 7,500 Jewish-owned stores and businesses, like Moshe's butcher shop and Mitzi Stein's seamstress shop in this story, were demolished. Local fire departments kept the blazes from spreading to German-owned buildings. Nearly every

synagogue in Germany suffered damage. The Neue Synagogue in Berlin was set on fire, but a local police chief prevented its total destruction by chasing away the gang of arsonists.

Approximately 100 Jews were killed, and hundreds more were hurt. About 30,000 arrests were made. People such as Professor Goldfarb, who in this story had tried to save Jewish books from the Nazi book burnings, were taken away to concentration camps. Some, like Sophie's family and Moshe the butcher, simply disappeared.

Only a few nations spoke out against the events of Kristallnacht, showing the Nazis that the world would tolerate the persecution of Jews on a mass scale. The Holocaust had begun.

BIBLIOGRAPHY

Sources

Read, Anthony and David Fisher. *Kristallnacht: The Nazi Night of Terror*, Random House, New York, 1989.

Schwab, Gerald. *The Day the Holocaust Began: The Odyssey of Herschel Grynszpan*, Praeger, New York, 1990.

Thalmann, Rita and Emmanuel Feinermann. *Crystal Night: A Gripping Documentary of the Nazi Night of Terror that was Prelude to the Holocaust*, Coward, McCann & Geoghegan, Inc., New York, 1974.

Additional Children's Books About the Holocaust

Abells, Chana Byers. *The Children We Remember*. New York: HarperTrophy, 2002.

Adler, David A. *The Number on my Grandfather's Arm*. New York, N.Y: UAHC, 1987.

Bunting, Eve. *Terrible Things: An Allegory of the Holocaust*. Philadelphia: Jewish Publication Society, 1993.

Gallaz, Christophe. *Rose Blanche*. New York: Creative Paperbacks Inc, 2005.

Hesse, Karen. *The Cats in Krasinski Square*. New York: Scholastic, 2004.

I Never Saw Another Butterfly: Children's Drawings And Poems From Terezin Concentration Camp, 1942-1944. New York: Schocken Books, 1993.

Lehman-Wilzig, Tami. Keeping *The Promise: A Torah's Journey*. Minneapolis, Minn: Kar-Ben Publishing, 2004.

Littlesugar, Amy. *Willy and Max: A Holocaust Story*. New York, N.Y: Philomel Books, 2005.

Polacco, Patricia. *The Butterfly*. New York: Philomel Books, 2000. Print.

MEG WIVIOTT grew up in New Jersey. She attended the University of Wisconsin where she majored in History, and earned a Master's degree in Education from Northwestern University. She is working on a Master's of Fine Arts degree at Vermont College of Fine Arts, in their Writing for Children and Young Adults program. Meg and her husband have two grown children and live in New Jersey. This is her first picture book.

JOSÉE BISAILLON grew up in St. Hyacinthe, Canada. Rather than following in her father's footsteps as a veterinary surgeon, she elected to make cut-paper animals: they were colorful, low maintenance and always in fine health. Her illustrations, focused on animals, are a mixture of collage, drawings and digital montage, creating a richly detailed and multi-dimensional world.